Colour CRACKERS

Read all the Colour CRACKERS books!

A Medal for **Poppy**

The Pluckiest Pig in the World!

Rose Impey and Shoo Rayner

1 84121 244 X

Too Many **Babies**

The Largest Litter in the World!

Rose Impey and Shoo Rayner

1 84121 242 3

Hot Dog **Harris**

The Smallest Dog in the World!

Rose Impey and Shoo Rayner

1 84121 232 6

Rhode Island **Roy**

The Roughest Rooster in the World!

Rose Impey and Shoo Rayner

1 84121 252 0

Welcome Home, **Barney**

The Loneliest Bat in the World!

Rose Impey and Shoo Rayner

1 84121 258 X

Pipe Down, **Prudle!**

The Most Talkative Parrot in the World!

Rose Impey and Shoo Rayner

1 84121 250 4

A Birthday for **Bluebell**

The Oldest Cow in the World!

Rose Impey and Shoo Rayner

1 84121 228 8

1 84121 240 7

1 84121 238 5

1 84121 248 2

1 84121 256 3

1 84121 236 9

1 84121 246 6

1 84121 230 X

1 84121 234 2

1 84121 254 7

A Medal for Poppy

The Pluckiest Pig in the World!

Rose Impey
Shoo Rayner

ORCHARD BOOKS

ORCHARD BOOKS
96 Leonard Street, London EC2A 4XD
Orchard Books Australia
32/45-51 Huntley Street, Alexandria, NSW 2015
First published in Great Britain in 1998
This edition published in hardback in 2003
This edition published in paperback in 2003
Text © Rose Impey 1998
Illustrations © Shoo Rayner 2003
The rights of Rose Impey to be identified as the author
and Shoo Rayner as the illustrator of this work
have been asserted by them in accordance with the
Copyright, Designs and Patents Act, 1988.
A CIP catalogue record for this book is
available from the British Library.
ISBN 1 84121 888 X (hardback)
ISBN 1 84121 244 X (paperback)
1 3 5 7 9 10 8 6 4 2 (hardback)
1 3 5 7 9 10 8 6 4 2 (paperback)
Printed in Hong Kong

A Medal for Poppy

Old Man Brocksopp had a farm,
Eee-Aye, Eee-Aye, *Yow!*
And on that farm he had two dogs,
and a sheep and a horse and a cow.

And a hen and a goose and a goat,
and a son called Dan,
with a wife called Nan,
and their little girl, Lucy-Anne.

And he also had a remarkable pig
called Poppy.

Everyone on the farm liked Poppy.
She was clever and kind
and very brave.

Sheep wasn't brave.
Sheep was scared of lots of things:
the farm dogs barking at her heels,

bright lights,

bang!

loud noises.

Even Sheep's shadow made
her shiver.

Oh, dear, oh, dear,
my poor old nerves.

"Fancy being
afraid of your
own shadow,"
thought Poppy.

Horse was braver than Sheep.
But even Horse hid his head
in the hay when there was
thunder and lightning.

"Fancy being afraid of the weather," thought Poppy.

Cow wasn't afraid of loud noises
or bright lights.
But Cow *was* afraid of the dark.
She didn't make a fuss about it.
She just moved up closer to her
friends when darkness came.

"Fancy being afraid of the dark," thought Poppy.

Poppy wasn't afraid of
bright lights
or loud noises
or being alone in the dark.
Poppy was a plucky pig.
Everybody said so.

They said so when Poppy chased the fox away when he tried to gobble up Goose's goslings!

They said so when she rescued
Cow from cattle rustlers.

You are t-o-o-o kind.

They said so when she saved Hen's eggs, the day the barn caught fire.

Poppy liked to do brave deeds.
She liked being told what a
plucky pig she was.

So brave.

Fearless!

But there *was* one thing Poppy
was afraid of:
Old Man Brocksopp's pond.

Once, when Poppy was a piglet,
she'd tried to walk on water.
And she'd never forgotten it.
So Poppy kept well away from
the farm pond.

Each day, when the sun was hot,
the other animals gathered round
the pond to feel the cool breeze
coming off the water.
But Poppy didn't join them.

If Poppy had to go on errands across the farm, she took the longest route, rather than pass by the pond.

No one seemed to notice.
No one guessed Poppy's secret.
Why would they?
After all, pigs don't swim, do they?

One day, Poppy had a nasty surprise.
Old Man Brocksopp was sitting in
the yard, reading his paper.

In the paper there was a picture
of a pig, just like her.
But this pig was swimming!
"What do you think of that?"
said the farmer.
Poppy didn't know what to
think of it.
But it made her blood run cold.

That night Poppy dreamed about
the swimming pig.
She woke up in a cold sweat.
And every night that week
she had the same dream.

Poppy didn't feel at all happy.
Everyone else still thought
she was a plucky pig.
But Poppy didn't feel plucky;
she *felt* scared.

She wanted to tell someone,
but she couldn't.
Then she thought of Goat.

Goat was old and wise.
Goat would help.
Poppy decided to talk to her.
Goat didn't seem at all surprised.
"Oh, my dear," she said.
"Everyone's scared of something."
"Are they?" said Poppy.

Of course. The brave animals are the ones who are scared - but don't show it. Like cow.

"Cow?" said Poppy.
"Yes," said Goat. "Cow hates the dark and she has to face it every night. That's what I call brave: knowing what you're afraid of, but *not* letting it get the better of you."

Poppy went away and thought
about Goat's words.
She knew what she had to do.
The next day Poppy went to join
her friends by the pond.
Each day she moved closer
and closer to the water,
until she didn't feel so afraid.

Monday

Tuesday

Wednesday

Thursday

Friday

33

It was quite a hard thing to do,
but Poppy didn't tell anyone.
It was her secret.

Slowly she began to feel brave again.
She began to feel like a plucky pig.
Then, one day, something terrible
happened.

All the animals were beside
the pond, as usual.

Old Man Brocksopp was in the
far field cutting the hay.

Dan was in the shed mending
the tractor.

Nan was in the farmhouse
paying the bills.

No one was watching little
Lucy-Anne.
No one noticed her
                toddling
                    across
                        the yard
                            heading
                                straight for
                                    the pond.

Poppy and all her friends were
snoozing in the midday sun.
Even the ducks were dreaming.
No one noticed little Lucy-Anne
trying to toddle on water.

But suddenly they heard her.
Suddenly everyone was wide awake.
Suddenly everyone went wild.

Waaaaah!

All the animals started up,
bleating and clucking
and mooing and neighing.
They didn't know what else to do,
so they all *panicked*.

But Poppy didn't panic.
She knew that someone
had to save the little girl.
Poppy, the plucky little pig,
who was *still afraid of water*,
jumped right in and
started to swim.

Poppy didn't know how she did it.
She just did it.
She kicked her little legs
and swam to the rescue.

Poppy opened her mouth
and fixed her teeth on
little Lucy-Anne's clothes
and towed her to the side.

The other animals had made
so much noise that everyone
had come running.
Nan was there,

and Dan was there.

Even Old Man Brocksopp
had heard them in the far field.
Everyone was there to see Poppy,
the pluckiest pig in the world,
save little Lucy-Anne from drowning.

Give that pig a medal.

None of them realised why this
was Poppy's bravest deed of all,
except Goat, of course.
And Goat knew how to keep a secret.

Crack-A-Joke

What do pigs use to
write to their friends?
Pen and oink!

What do you give a sick pig?
Oinkment!

What do you call a
story about pigs?
A pig tail!

Waiter, this stew
isn't fit for a pig!

Would sir like me
to take it away
and fetch him
some that is?

What happens when pigs fly?
The price of bacon goes up!

Why is getting up at
three o'clock in the
morning like a pig's tail?
It's twirly.

What do you call a
thief that breaks into
a hamburger factory?
A hamburglar!

There are 16 Colour Crackers books.
Collect them all!

❏ A Birthday for Bluebell	1 84121 228 8	£3.99
❏ A Fortune for Yo-Yo	1 84121 230 X	£3.99
❏ A Medal for Poppy	1 84121 244 X	£3.99
❏ Hot Dog Harris	1 84121 232 6	£3.99
❏ Long Live Roberto	1 84121 246 6	£3.99
❏ Open Wide, Wilbur	1 84121 248 2	£3.99
❏ Phew, Sidney!	1 84121 234 2	£3.99
❏ Pipe Down, Prudle!	1 84121 250 4	£3.99
❏ Precious Potter	1 84121 236 9	£3.99
❏ Rhode Island Roy	1 84121 252 0	£3.99
❏ Sleepy Sammy	1 84121 238 5	£3.99
❏ Stella's Staying Put	1 84121 254 7	£3.99
❏ Tiny Tim	1 84121 240 7	£3.99
❏ Too Many Babies	1 84121 242 3	£3.99
❏ We Want William!	1 84121 256 3	£3.99
❏ Welcome Home, Barney	1 84121 258 X	£3.99

Colour Crackers are available from all good bookshops,
or can be ordered direct from the publisher:
Orchard Books, PO BOX 29, Douglas IM99 1BQ
Credit card orders please telephone 01624 836000 or fax 01624 837033
or e-mail: bookshop@enterprise.net for details.
To order please quote title, author and ISBN and your full name and address.
Cheques and postal orders should be made payable to 'Bookpost plc'.
Postage and packing is FREE within the UK
(overseas customers should add £1.00 per book).
Prices and availability are subject to change.

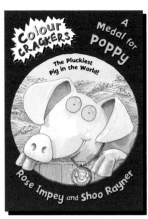

1 84121 244 X

1 84121 240 7

1 84121 238 5

1 84121 252 0

1 84121 256 3

1 84121 236 9

1 84121 228 8

1 84121 230 X

1 84121 234 2

1 84121 248 2

1 84121 242 3

1 84121 232 6

1 84121 246 6

1 84121 258 X

1 84121 250 4

1 84121 254 7

Read all the Colour CRACKERS books!

Collect all the
Colour Crackers!